The Author

Stephanie Dagg lives in Innishannon, County Cork.

She is married to Chris and is a mother of two children, Benjamin and Caitlín, and has been writing stories ever since she was a child. Originally from Suffolk in England, she moved to Cork in 1992.

Contents

Chapter 1   Re-Witched   7

Chapter 2   Broom and Big Roddy   17

Chapter 3   Blooming Cats   23

Chapter 4   Spelling Test   31

Chapter 5   Carol Cackles Again   38

1 Re-Witched

Someone was searching for a broom and a dog. This someone had neatly cut hair, a trendy outfit, a suitcase with some scrubbed spell bottles and books — and a broken heart. This someone was Cackling Carol.

Cackling Carol was a witch — or rather she used to be a witch. That had all ended after she had been taken from her cavern several months ago by some well-meaning social workers and rehoused in a flat. Her new neighbour, Flo, had introduced her to shopping and the cinema, and gradually Cackling Carol had been de-witched. She had forgotten all about her trusty friends, Broom — her broom, of course — and Big Roddy, her witch's dog. (Cackling Carol hated cats so that's why she'd got Big Roddy from the dog's home a year or so ago.)

This morning, while she had been out on yet another shopping trip, Big Roddy and Broom had left the flat, fed up at being on their own all the time.

Cackling Carol had discovered that they had gone when she got back, weighed down with shopping bags. She realised, to her shame, that she had neglected them and betrayed them. She also realised just how much she loved her two companions. But too late! They were gone.

Cackling Carol had had a good cry but then pulled herself together.

'Silly me!' she had scolded herself. 'I must go and find them. And I will find them, even if it takes for ever!' With that, she had quickly packed her things and set off, leaving the hated flat and the dreadful Flo behind.

At the end of the street she stopped and put her heavy suitcase down on the ground. Where should she look first? She thought for a

Witching Again!

moment or two. Their old cavern of course! Surely they'd have gone there. Carol grabbed her suitcase and was about to set off towards the edge of town when a blue double-decker bus pulled up next to her.

'Do you want to get on, love?' called the driver. Cackling Carol looked up and saw that she was standing next to a bus stop sign. Now Carol had never been on a bus, even though she had always really wanted to. She'd seen them around often enough when she'd been out shopping with Flo. But whenever she had suggested that they go for a bus ride, Flo had turned up her nose and said 'no'! Flo always preferred taking a taxi.

But Carol was on her own now and here was her chance to ride on a bus! She had a bit of money left in her pocket so she struggled onto the bus with her suitcase.

'Where do you want to go?' asked the driver.

Carol didn't know what to say.

'Well?' The driver was sounding impatient now.

Carol pulled a pound coin out of her pocket.

'How far can I go for this?' she asked.

'Quite a long way,' smiled the driver, taking the money and giving her a ticket. 'That'll take you to the heath at the edge of town. Is that OK?'

That was perfect. It was in the right direction for getting home.

Cackling Carol dumped her case in the luggage area and clambered up the stairs to the top storey. Luckily the very front seats were empty. She plonked herself down happily on one of them to enjoy the ride.

But it was terrifying! Every time the bus turned a corner, Carol was sure that they were going to crash into the cars coming towards them. The bus seemed to swing so far out!

And when they approached a low bridge, Cackling Carol dived under her seat. She was convinced they were going to hit it! This was far scarier than riding Broom. Oh dear, she shouldn't have thought about Broom. A big fat tear trickled down her cheek.

Looking round for something to cheer her up, she spotted a button with 'push' on it.

So Cackling Carol pushed it. A bell sounded. Carol pushed it again. Again the bell sounded.

This is fun! thought Carol. She pressed the button several more times until the driver's voice rose angrily up the stairs. 'Stop pushing that bell, madam!' he snapped. Carol stopped at once.

They were soon at the heath. Cackling Carol collected her case and climbed off the bus. The driver was glad to see her go!

After walking for a long, long time, Cackling Carol reached her woods, just as dusk was falling. She dived into them. She pushed through bramble bushes and waded through bogs in her hurry to get back home and find Broom and Big Roddy. Her neat hair got tangled and scragged by branches. Her outfit got torn and muddy. She began to look a bit more like a witch again. And as she battled through the undergrowth, she started to remember some of her spells. She'd always been too busy shopping and going to the cinema to think of them while she'd been living in the flat. Chanting some of the old magic words and phrases again cheered her up. Witching was far more fun than watching films or waiting in queues at the cash till in shops.

Now Cackling Carol felt like a proper witch. She turned a couple of spiders into lizards and felt even better. She spotted a tiny mouse being chased by an owl and, with a click of her fingers, made the mouse the size of a hare. The startled owl hooted in horror and streaked off. The mouse looked round in surprise but then trotted off happily enough.

Carol chuckled to herself. She was still chuckling when she reached her cavern. But then she stopped and stared in horror. Her cave was all boarded up! And there was a big sign nailed to the boards.

'Danger, no entry,' she read aloud. 'Danger indeed! How could my cosy old home be dangerous, I should like to know?' She bristled with anger. 'What have you done to my old home?' She thumped helplessly at the strong boards.

Then she saw a hole at the bottom right hand corner. 'What's this?' she wondered. She bent to have a closer look and caught sight of what looked like a ball of fluff stuck to the edges of the broken boards. She pulled it off. She recognised the feel of it at once. It was Big Roddy's fur! So he'd been here, and recently too. She was hot on the trail of Broom and Big Roddy.

'Hooray!' she trilled. She didn't stop to look around her old home, not that there was anything to see anyway. Grasping the handful of Big Roddy's fur, she recited a tracking spell. At once a glowing green path appeared, showing her where the former owner of the fur had gone. With new energy, Cackling Carol jogged along, her suitcase of bottles clanking alarmingly. She soon saw that the path was leading to Witch Matilda's cavern. Witch Matilda was the head of the coven of witches that Cackling Carol was in — which just means that Matilda was her boss!

'Clever Broom! Clever Big Roddy,' she smiled. What a sensible thing to do, to go and see Witch Matilda. With any luck they'd still be there. Carol started to run. The bottles clanked even more and then started to crack and splinter.

'Whoops!' exclaimed Carol, slowing down for an instant, then, 'Oh, who cares!' she shouted as she threw the case down. She could always get new bottles and spell books but she couldn't get a new Broom or Big Roddy. They were far more important.

2 Broom and Big Roddy

Meanwhile, not too far ahead, Broom and Big Roddy were nearly at Witch Matilda's. The two friends had been travelling for hours and they were tired and hungry. In fact, Big Roddy was starving. He'd only had a few berries all day. His tummy was starting to rumble. Suddenly a rabbit jumped out onto the path just in front of him. Big Roddy stiffened. He knew what rabbits were. He'd seen pictures of them on tins of dog food. Here was dinner!

With a mighty woof, Big Roddy lunged towards the rabbit. The rabbit turned and fled. Big Roddy chased after it.

'Come back, Big Roddy!' shouted Broom, rushing off after his hairy friend. 'You'll never catch it.'

At that moment, the rabbit reached its burrow and dived in. Big Roddy dived in too, but as he was so big, only his head could get in. Big Roddy gave a startled yelp and tried to pull his head out. But it wouldn't budge.

He was stuck.

Broom arrived at the scene.

'Oh, you silly dog,' he exclaimed when he saw Big Roddy's bottom waving in the air. 'How am I going to get you out?'

Broom tried tugging on Big Roddy's tail but that just made the poor dog yelp.

'Whoops! Sorry,' apologised Broom.

Then, using his hands, he scraped away at the burrow entrance to try and widen it. Big Roddy helped by scrabbling away with his big paws. After ten minutes or so, Big Roddy at last pulled his head free. His ears were full of dirt and his nose was covered in mud, but apart from that he was fine. He was just a bit ashamed of doing such a daft thing!

'Come on,' said Broom, ducking the grit and gravel that flew everywhere as Big Roddy shook himself. 'Let's get to Matilda's.'

They carried on through the woods and soon arrived at Witch Matilda's cavern. She was waiting for them. She'd spotted them coming in her crystal ball.

'Well, well, well, this is nice,' cackled Witch Matilda ushering them inside. 'Broom — and Big Roddy, the wizard catcher!

Come in, come in, my dears. You'd better tell me everything that's happened to you. I heard that our Carol had been witchnapped. Goodness me, what a wicked world it is when witches can't be left in peace and quiet any more.'

'I quite agree, madam,' said Broom politely. 'But first, please could you give Big Roddy some supper. He's had nothing but a few berries all day and is starving.'

'Of course, of course, my dear,' nodded Matilda. She bustled off to make a tasty stew for Big Roddy. But first she cleared the cats from the rug in front of her fire so that Big Roddy could collapse there. The cats muttered angrily and hissed at the huge dog, but he was too exhausted to care. He managed a feeble wag of his tail to say 'thank you' but the cats ignored it. Witch's cats really are very disagreeable animals.

Matilda was soon back with a bowl piled high with, well, something or other for Big Roddy that smelled very tempting. Big Roddy cheered up at once at the sight of the meal and wolfed it down in seconds. Matilda listened in horror as Broom told her the tale of what had happened to them all, and most especially of how Cackling Carol had been de-witched.

'To think our Carol would actually get her fingernails cut!' gasped Witch Matilda.

21

'And her hair done! And even start wearing trouser suits. Cat's whiskers! What have they done to her?' Matilda shook her head sadly. 'Never mind, my dears,' she went on. 'You can live here with me for as long as you need. There's plenty of room in my cave.'

That was true enough. Because she was head of the coven, Matilda had a huge home. It had a long, deep passage that extended far into the hillside. At the very end of this passage stood a large earthenware jar. Its sides were very thick, but if you listened carefully you could hear someone shouting angrily inside it. That's because in this jar was Egbert, the blue wizard — the one that Big Roddy had caught not so very long ago. After Big Roddy had caught Egbert, Matilda and the other witches had sealed him into this large jar for a thousand years. It served Egbert right — he was a very, very nasty piece of work.

3 Blooming Cats

Broom felt quite happy to be with Matilda. It was so nice to be back in a dusty, cobwebby, gloomy cavern. Carol's clean, sparkling flat had been almost too much to bear. But soon Big Roddy was not so happy. Matilda's seven cats were being horrid. They kept spitting at him and lashing out with their claws when their mistress wasn't looking. They always seemed to get his nose and it was getting very sore indeed.

And he'd just found out that more cats would be arriving soon. He heard Witch Matilda tell Broom that she was holding a meeting of her coven that very night.

'We shall talk about how to get Cackling Carol back,' Matilda promised. 'I was going to give a lecture on lizard skinning techniques, but that can wait.'

Big Roddy wagged his tail at that news.

Soon the witches — and their cats — were all gathered at Matilda's cavern. Witch Matilda called them to order by rapping a lizard's skull on her chair.

'Now, now, sisters,' she screeched. 'Settle down.'

The witches, who had all been catching up with the latest gossip, coughed and muttered for a little bit longer but finally fell silent.

Witch Matilda stood up. 'I've decided to postpone my lecture,' she told them. There was a huge sigh of relief. 'There is something more important to talk about tonight. As you may know, our sister Cackling Carol was cruelly dragged from her home and taken to some terrible, clean place where she was de-witched!'

There were gasps of horror.

'She has abandoned her broom and her faithful, wizard-catching dog. No witch in her right mind would betray her closest friends in this way.'

There were murmurs of 'Absolutely not' and 'Disgusting' and 'How terrible!'

'The time has come to find our sister and rescue her. Now, how shall we do this?' asked Matilda.

The witches had plenty of ideas.

'How about sending a plague of frogs into the town to scare all the do-gooders away?'

'Why not raid all the homes in the area one by one until we find Cackling Carol? We could send in spiders as spies.'

'Let's make Cackling Carol invisible. She'll get so fed up being ignored she'll come home again.'

Broom listened but Big Roddy was too fed up to pay attention. He was beginning to think he would never see Cackling Carol again.

And besides, Matilda's cats were starting to tease him again. Some of the other cats were joining in. They took it in turns to sneak up behind him and stick their claws into his tail or his bottom. One of them even knocked his witch's hat off!

That got Big Roddy very cross. He began to growl but that just made the cats sillier. They got more daring and began to pull his ears and jump on his paws. The bravest cat then stole Big Roddy's hat and went tearing off down the passage with it.

This was too much! Big Roddy charged after the giggling cat. The other cats joined in the fun. They tossed Big Roddy's hat one to another. Big Roddy was frantic. Cackling Carol had given him that hat in the good old days. He treasured it above anything else. Those nasty cats would surely wreck it.

Big Roddy did everything he could to catch the cats but they were just too quick.

By now they had come to the end of the passage where the jar containing Egbert stood. The smallest cat now had the hat in its mouth and was running round and round the jar, hotly pursued by Big Roddy and the other cats. Getting dizzier and dizzier, Big Roddy lunged at the cat. But he missed it. Instead he landed on the jar. Now the jar was big and heavy — but Big Roddy was even bigger and heavier. The jar wobbled, then it rocked, then it swayed from side to side until . . . SMASH! it crashed to the floor and shattered into a thousand pieces. Big Roddy froze. There was a flash of blue lightning and a blue whirlwind hurtled down the passageway towards the witches. Wizard Egbert was loose!

The cats didn't wait around to see what would happen. They just ran for it. Big Roddy was still too scared to move. Then he felt his tail being tugged. Broom had seen the blue flash and guessed what had happened.

He'd come straight away to get his friend out of danger.

'Quickly!' hissed Broom. 'We've got to get out of here and away from Egbert. Hold on to me as tightly as you can.'

Big Roddy sank the claws of his front paws into Broom's bristles. The pair of them looked very funny as Big Roddy ran along on his back paws while Broom, waving his arms madly, tried to fly but only managed to drag himself and Big Roddy along a few centimetres above the ground. But there was no-one to laugh at them. Egbert had just turned all the witches and their cats to stone in revenge for them putting him in the jar. He didn't see Big Roddy and Broom escape into the night.

He laughed nastily at the sight of the witch and cat statues.

'Serves you right! No-one messes with the great Egbert and gets away with it,' he cried.

'But I see that the one they call Cackling Carol isn't here, nor is her monstrous mutt, that Big Roddy. I shall have to find them. They're not going to get away from me.'

And with that he stormed out of the cavern, sweeping his sapphire-blue cape around him. His bright blue eyes glistened with hatred.

4 Spelling Test

Cackling Carol wasn't far from Matilda's cavern now, following Big Roddy's glowing trail. But as she got closer, she began to slow down. It wasn't just that she was getting tired from so much walking and running (Cackling Carol wasn't very fit). It was also that she was beginning to wonder if Broom and Big Roddy would be pleased to see her. They might not want to come back to her.

'I wouldn't blame them,' thought Carol sadly. 'I was really rotten.'

She sat down on a sleeping badger and had a little cry. She didn't notice what seemed to be a blue shooting star flash through the sky above her. But the star noticed her.

'Now, now, this will never do,' Carol told herself firmly, blowing her nose on the sleeve of her silk blouse. 'I will find Broom and Big Roddy and ask them to forgive me. And if they won't, well, I shall have only myself to blame.'

She squared her shoulders and marched on until she came to the entrance of Witch Matilda's cavern. It seemed very quiet although Carol could see that a fire was burning inside.

'Matilda, it's Cackling Carol!' she called. 'I'm a witch again!'

No reply. Not even a cat appeared.

'Matilda, are you there?'

Still nothing.

Cautiously Carol stepped into the cavern. She looked around. There were plates of delicious beetle biscuits and bowls of fly jelly on the table. Clearly Witch Matilda was planning a party. But where was everyone?

Carol turned into the room where they usually had their meetings — and shrieked! There stood her sister witches, and their cats — but all turned to stone!

'There's only one person who can do magic this powerful,' Cackling Carol exclaimed out loud.

'Yes, me!' came a voice from behind her. Carol whirled round to see Wizard Egbert looking very pleased with himself.

Cackling Carol's jaw dropped in amazement.

'Ha ha!' Egbert gloated. 'You weren't expecting to see me for another nine hundred and ninety-nine years were you? You thought I was still in that jar, didn't you? Well, surprise, surprise. Here I am. And I've been looking for you.'

'Oh?' said Carol in a very wobbly voice. She was horrified.

'Yes, and that monstrous mutt of yours.

You two were responsible for me getting caught, weren't you?' Egbert looked very threatening.

'No, no, it was just me. All my idea. My dog just did what I told him,' gabbled Cackling Carol. The least she could do was to try and keep Big Roddy out of trouble.

'Nonsense! That dastardly dog is as guilty as you are. I'll find him, don't you worry. I found you, didn't I? Now, what shall I do with you. Something very nasty I think!' Egbert laughed unpleasantly and began to pace round and round Carol.

Come on, come on, think of something, you silly witch! Carol scolded herself. Now was the time to act, while Egbert was off guard.

Suddenly a spell plopped into her brain. Her favourite spell! It turned people into toads. It might work on wizards too.

She shrieked out a few weird words and suddenly there was a fat blue toad hopping around her. But only for a few seconds. Egbert was a powerful magician. He quickly undid Carol's spell by turning it back on her. Now Cackling Carol was the toad!

'I'll squash you, you cackling toad,' grinned Egbert, trying to stamp on Cackling Carol. Carol leapt here, there and everywhere to avoid his big blue boots. As she did, she croaked out a few more magic words. These made up the 'turn into a fly' spell.

Before her toady eyes, Egbert shrunk and turned into a fly. Carol the toad knew what to do. She shot out her tongue and wrapped it round the very blue bluebottle. But before she could swallow Egbert and so destroy him for ever, he reversed the spell she had cast on him. Carol found herself stuck with a full size Egbert sitting on her tongue. It hurt!

Witching Again!

'Now I've got you, puny witch,' chuckled Egbert.

Huh! No-one calls me puny and gets away with it, thought Carol angrily. Summoning up her magic powers, she undid the toad spell just as Egbert reached out to grab her. He ended up with a handful of curly hair. He gave it a spiteful tug.

'Ouch!' cried Carol, loudly. 'You're a rotten bully, Egbert.'

She turned him into a cat. Egbert turned her into a mouse. Quickly Carol turned Egbert into a piece of cheese. Egbert turned Carol into a mousetrap. And so it went on, each of them turning the other into lots of different things.

'This could be a long fight,' thought Carol to herself wearily.

5 Carol Cackles Again

Broom and Big Roddy weren't far away.
They were hiding near Witch Matilda's
cave, hoping that Egbert wouldn't find them.
They huddled together.

Suddenly Big Roddy sat upright, pricking
his big floppy ears as much as he could.

'Get down!' hissed Broom, pulling at Big
Roddy's collar. 'Egbert will see us!'

But Big Roddy wouldn't get down. He
began to whimper excitedly.

'What is it, Big Roddy?' asked Broom,
giving up the battle. 'What can you hear?'

Big Roddy had heard Cackling Carol say
'Ouch!' as Egbert pulled her hair. Well, he
thought it was Cackling Carol. He hoped it
was. No, on second thoughts he was positive
it was Carol. He jumped up to find his
mistress.

'Where are you going?' gasped Broom, grabbing Big Roddy's tail to stop him. Had he gone crazy? Why did he want to risk getting caught by Egbert? Broom would only risk such a thing for Cackling Carol but —

'Good gracious!' cried Broom, suddenly understanding. 'You heard Cackling Carol didn't you? Clever dog. Come on, let's find her — before Egbert does, if we can.'

Big Roddy charged off towards Matilda's cave again, closely followed by Broom. They arrived at the doorway just in time to see a blue octopus turning a sea horse into a crab.

Both fishy creatures turned to stare at them. In an instant the octopus became a wizard and the crab became Cackling Carol. There was delight on Carol's face for a moment but it quickly changed into concern.

'Run, Big Roddy! Fly, Broom! Get away from here!' she cried in warning.

'Too late!' chirped Egbert, gleefully conjuring up a blue brick wall to block the entrance to the cave. 'No-one's going anywhere!'

It was true. They were all trapped.

Cackling Carol began to try and magic the wall away but this time she couldn't undo Egbert's spell.

'I've got the lot of you,' smirked Egbert. 'Who shall I dispose of first, I wonder? Oh, silly me, how could I forget. Ladies first! No messing around this time, my dear. Say goodbye to your doggy and your floor cleaner.'

He drew back his arm to cast a dreadful spell on Cackling Carol but Broom threw himself at the wizard and began bashing him about the head.

'Leave Cackling Carol alone,' he yelled.

There was a blue flash. Broom disappeared. In his place sat a floor cloth.

Then Big Roddy leapt into the fray. With a piercing howl he jumped at the wizard and knocked him down. But the next moment, Egbert picked himself up and threw a small toy dog to the ground beside him. This toy dog had a tiny witch's hat. It was Big Roddy.

Carol watched in dismay. Her dear friends, who she'd betrayed so terribly, had tried to save her. They hadn't thought of themselves at all. They were brave and noble. They were friends indeed! And Egbert had defeated them and made them look silly. Cackling Carol was furious.

With every shred of her magic powers she screamed the most powerful spell she knew at the smug wizard. She wasn't sure it would work but it was worth a try. Egbert was caught completely by surprise. Next instant, instead of a blue wizard there was a blue personal computer, complete with screen and printer, in front of her. And because there was no electricity in the cavern, the computer couldn't work. And because it couldn't work, Egbert couldn't do anything. Carol had done it! She'd beaten Egbert!

But at a cost. She was drained. She sank to her knees. Her magic was almost all gone. She only had a little bit left.

First she turned Broom back from a floor cloth. He zoomed to her side and Carol gave him a weak hug.

'Dear Broom,' she croaked. 'Dear friend.'

Broom sniffed and wiped his eyes. 'Oh mistress, thank goodness you're safe!'

Then she turned to Big Roddy. She opened her mouth to say the spell to transform him, but before she could do so, a shimmering pink haze filled the cave around her. The pink haze gradually took the form of a hooded face. It was the Witch Spirit. Cackling Carol had only ever seen the Witch Spirit once before, when she first became a witch. The Witch Spirit was the source of every witch's magic. She only appeared at times of great importance.

'Cackling Carol,' said the figure.

'Yes, oh great Witch Spirit?' whispered Cackling Carol.

'Carol, my child, your powers are almost gone. Battling with the great wizard has used up all your magic.'

'I know,' nodded Cackling Carol.

'If you cast your next spell, you will exhaust your powers completely. You will never do magic again.' The Witch Spirit sounded grave but kind. 'So what will you do, my child?'

Carol didn't hesitate. 'I must cast the spell, Witch Spirit. I have to.'

'I understand,' sighed the Witch Spirit. 'And I will help you. But this will be your last spell.' With that, the Witch Spirit vanished.

Cackling Carol didn't care. Big Roddy was worth losing her magic for. There was no contest — Big Roddy meant all the magic in the world to her.

She uttered the spell. The toy dog became a big, slobbering bundle of fur with a witch's hat. He bounded over to Carol and licked her joyfully. Cackling Carol hugged him with her remaining strength.

'I'm sorry, boys,' she whispered to him and Broom. 'Will you forgive me?'

'I think they already have!' came a voice. Carol looked up. It was Witch Matilda!

When Cackling Carol had broken Egbert's spell over Roddy, the Witch Spirit had broken his enchantment of the witches too. They were statues no longer and they had a lot to say!

'Carol, you're back!'

'We've missed you, dear.'

'My, look at those horrible clean nails.'

'Whatever are you wearing?'

'Egbert's done for this time. Well done!'

'Yes, Egbert the computer will make a very nice footstool for Matilda. Such a nice shade of blue.'

'I hope Egbert catches some nasty computer viruses.'

'Goodness, Carol, what short hair!'

The witches helped Cackling Carol to Matilda's bed. Broom and Big Roddy stuck close. Carol was very, very weak. Matilda went to fetch some nourishing frog soup and stinging nettle tea, with extra stings.

'So the Witch Spirit appeared, did she?' she asked when she returned with a loaded tray.

Cackling Carol nodded. 'I shall have to leave your coven now, I suppose. I have no magic left at all,' she croaked sadly.

'Well, I wouldn't be so sure about that,' replied Witch Matilda, winking. 'I know a trick or two. With a little luck, we should be able to get some of your powers restored, but probably not for a couple of thousand years. Still, there's no hurry is there?'

There certainly wasn't. It was more than enough for Cackling Carol just to be back with Big Roddy and Broom again. When she was better, she'd search for a new, hidden cavern somewhere where no-one could ever possibly find them. Carol knew she'd get by quite happily without her magic spells just so long as she had her friends with her.

'Because friends,' she smiled at Broom and Big Roddy, 'are really magic.'